Country File
Brazil

Marion Morrison

Å⁺
Smart Apple Media

First published in 2003 by Franklin Watts
96 Leonard Street, London EC2A 4XD, UK

Franklin Watts Australia
45–51 Huntley Street, Alexandria, NSW 2015

Country File: Brazil produced for Franklin Watts by Bender
Richardson White, PO Box 266, Uxbridge, UK.

Editor: Lionel Bender, *Designer and Page Make-up:* Ben
White, *Picture Researcher:* Cathy Stastny, *Cover Make-up:*
Mike Pilley, Radius, *Production:* Kim Richardson, *Graphics
and Maps:* Stefan Chabluk
Copyright © 2003 Bender Richardson White

Consultant: Dr. Terry Jennings, a former geography teacher
and university lecturer. He is now a full-time writer of
children's geography and science books.

Published in the United States by Smart Apple Media
1980 Lookout Drive, North Mankato, Minnesota 56003

Library of Congress Cataloging-in-Publication Data

Morrison, Marion. Brazil / by Marion Morrison.
p. cm. — (Country files) Includes index.
Contents: Welcome to Brazil — The land — The people —
Urban and rural life — Farming and fishing — Resources
and industry — Transport — Education — Sports and leisure —
Daily life and religion — Arts and media — Government —
Place in the world.
ISBN 1-58340-235-7   1. Brazil—Juvenile literature.
[1. Brazil.] I. Title. II. Series.
F2508.5.M67 2003   981.06'4—dc21   2003042754

9 8 7 6 5 4 3 2 1

The Author
Marion Morrison is a writer and editor
of books about the countries of South
America. With her photographer
husband, Tony Morrison, she runs the
photo library *South American Pictures*.

Contents

Welcome to Brazil

Brazil is the largest country in South America. It is almost the same size as the United States. Brazil is famous for its huge forests, colorful carnivals, and championship soccer team.

On the east, its 4,970-mile (8,000 km) long Atlantic coastline has landscapes ranging from golden beaches to wild swamps. The Amazon River crosses Brazil at the equator from west to east. To the north, west, and south, Brazil borders 10 other South American countries.

Brazilians have their origins in many races. Almost 500 years ago, Portuguese settlers arrived from Europe and intermarried with the Native Americans. Many years later, other people landed from such places as Italy, the Netherlands, West Africa, and Japan. Today, most Brazilians speak Portuguese. Brazil is quickly becoming one of the world's most vibrant and multicultural nations.

Brazil is a young person's country. Music is everywhere; movies, books, and magazines abound. Televison has an enormous audience and reaches even distant parts of the Amazon forests.

Brazilians and tourists alike relax on Copacabana beach and swim in the Atlantic Ocean at Rio de Janeiro. ▼
▼

70°W   60°W   50°W   40°W

10°N

VENEZUELA

GUYANA

SURINAME

FRENCH GUIANA

COLOMBIA

Boa Vista

Amapá

Macapá

Pico da Neblina

Brancos

Negro

Amazon

0°

Belém

São Luis

Fortaleza

Fernando de Noronha

Atol das Rocas

Japurá

Manaus

Santarém

Solimões

Madeira

Tapajós

Xingu

Tocantins

Marabá

Teresina

Juruá

Purus

Porto Velho

Parnaiba

Recife

Rio Branco

São Francisco

Maceió

PERU

Barragem de Sobradinho

Juazeiro

10°S

B R A Z I L

Salvador

PLANALTO DE

MINAS GERAIS

Cuiabá

M A T O   G R O S S O

BRASILIA

Montes Claros

BOLIVIA

SERRA DA CANASTRA

Campo Grande

São José do Rio Preto

Paraná

Belo Horizonte

20°S

PARAGUAY

São Paulo

Rio de Janeiro

Itaipú

Santos

Tropic of Cancer

CHILE

Iguaçu Falls

Curitiba

SERRA DO MAR

ATLANTIC

Uruguay

OCEAN

30°S

ARGENTINA

Pôrto Alegre

URUGUAY

PACIFIC OCEAN

ATLANTIC

OCEAN

Mountains	△	Mountain peak
Grassland and farming		
▢ Capital	○	Major city
Country boundary		

0   1,000 Miles

0   1,000 Kilometers

The Land

A t its widest point, Brazil stretches 2,690 miles (4,330 km) from east to west. From north to south, the longest distance is 2,685 miles (4,320 km). The highest point is 9,888 feet (3,014 m), on *Pico da Neblina*, the forested "Peak of Mists" in the northern state of Amazonas.

In such a large country, no one region can be thought of as average. Parts of the northeast are so dry that in some years people have to migrate to find water. In contrast, some parts of the southern coast suffer from floods every year. There is often frost in the south, and occasionally it snows. Landslides due to summer rain are frequent on the hills surrounding the beautiful coastal city of Rio de Janeiro.

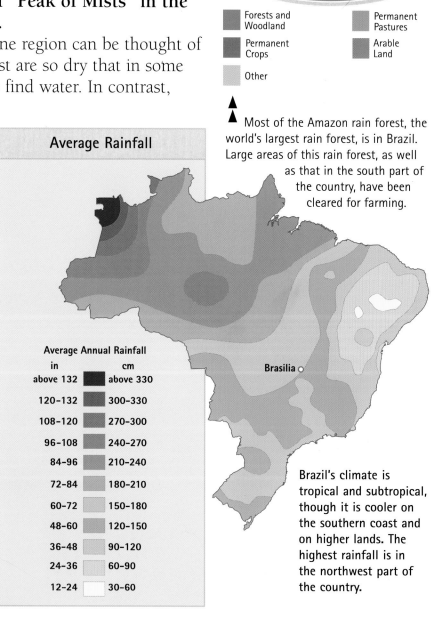

22% 1% 5%
14%
58%

Forests and Woodland

Permanent Pastures

Permanent Crops

Arable Land

Other

Most of the Amazon rain forest, the world's largest rain forest, is in Brazil. Large areas of this rain forest, as well as that in the south part of the country, have been cleared for farming.

Average Rainfall

Average Annual Rainfall

in		cm
above 132		above 330
120–132		300–330
108–120		270–300
96–108		240–270
84–96		210–240
72–84		180–210
60–72		150–180
48–60		120–150
36–48		90–120
24–36		60–90
12–24		30–60

Brasilia ○

Brazil's climate is tropical and subtropical, though it is cooler on the southern coast and on higher lands. The highest rainfall is in the northwest part of the country.

Time Zones

Brazil has three time zones, each one hour apart. The easternmost zone is three hours behind Greenwich Mean Time, so when it is 6:00 A.M. in London, it is 3:00 A.M. in Rio de Janeiro. The clocks on Fernando de Noronha, a group of 19 small islands 214 miles (345 km) from the coast, are one hour ahead of Rio.

 The Iguaçu Falls form part of the border between Brazil and Argentina. This section is known as the Deodoro Falls. The Iguaçu River is a tributary of the Paraná River.

Animals

The Amazon rain forest contains a greater number of plant species than any other habitat on earth, and Brazil's forests contain thousands of different species of plants and animals. The largest mammal is the tapir, a pig-like animal that is in fact a relative of the horse. It can weigh up to 550 pounds (250 kg). The smallest mammals are rodents that weigh as little as .7 ounce (20 g).

One Amazon catfish, the *piraiba*, can weigh more than 440 pounds (200 kg). A parrot of the northeast, Spix's macaw, is the rarest bird in the world. It inhabits the dry scrub grasslands known as the *caatinga*, but is believed to have become extinct in the wild in July 2002.

Rivers and landscape

Almost half of Brazil is dominated by the Amazon River. It has thousands of tributary rivers, although not all begin within the country's boundaries. Not all the banks of the Amazon are forested. Some are swampy, while other banks are grasslands or dry scrub.

In southwest Brazil, the Paraná River is also a giant. It gathers water from 11 percent of the country, then flows south to the sea through Argentina. Rainfall in this region of Brazil is so heavy that dams on the Paraná are able to generate enormous hydroelectric power.

The only major river that is totally Brazilian is the 1,965-mile (3,161 km) long São Francisco. It rises in the Serra da Canastra northwest of Rio de Janeiro and flows northward through a region that in places is almost a desert. The river is used for irrigating farmland.

 Web Search ▶▶

▶ http://www.ibge.gov.br
A huge database of information about the country, from the Brazilian Institute of Geography and Statistics; there is an option to read the information in English.

The People

The population of Brazil is increasing by approximately three million people each year. By the end of 2002, the population was estimated at 175,572,385. About half the people are less than 25 years old.

Most Brazilians are descended from European ancestry, and some of the immigrant communities still retain their own identity. Swiss-Germans settled in forested mountains to the northeast of Rio de Janeiro in 1819. Germans began to arrive in 1824 and headed to the cooler south. The main German towns are in the southern states of Rio Grande do Sul and Santa Catarina.

Arabs, Lebanese, and Syrians arrived between 1860 and 1890 and worked in the rubber trade in the Amazon region, where today many shops have names of Middle Eastern origin. Japanese immigrants first settled in São Paulo in 1908 and started to cultivate land. Later, some Japanese moved into other jobs, and now they are the most prosperous of all the ethnic groups.

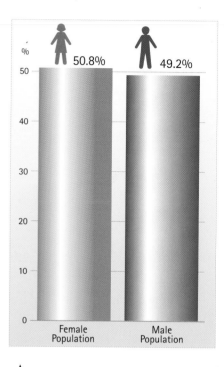

▲ The proportion of males and females in the Brazilian population.

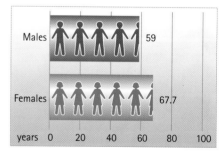

▲ A comparison of the average life expectancy of males and females in Brazil.

◄◄ Mestiço street vendors selling food in the coastal town of Salvador.

Population

The population of Brazil is concentrated in the south and along the coast, away from the dense northern rain forests.

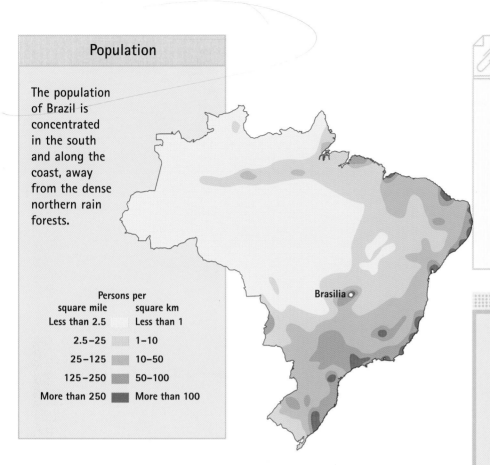

Persons per	
square mile	square km
Less than 2.5	Less than 1
2.5–25	1–10
25–125	10–50
125–250	50–100
More than 250	More than 100

Brasilia o

Language

Brazilians speak Portuguese but with some differences from the language of Portugal. For example, *taxi* means taxicab, but in Brazil it is also the word used in the northeast for an ant tree or the ants living in the stalks of the tree's leaves.

DATABASE

Japanese generations

The Japanese of São Paulo keep their traditional name for each generation, or *sei*. First-generation immigrants were the *issei*. Second-generation are the *nissei*. Third-generation are *sansei*. Fourth-generation are *yonsei*.

Web Search ▶▶

▶ http://www.funai.gov.br
National Indian Foundation/ Fundação Nacional do Indio has information about the Native Americans in Portuguese.

▶ http://www.ibge.gov.br
The Brazilian Institute of Geography and Statistics Web site has a "population clock" updated monthly.

The Native Americans and *mestiçoes*

In the early 16th century, explorers called the country "The Land of Brazil" after a wood found there that had the color of glowing embers, or *brasa* in Portuguese. At that time, there are thought to have been well over two million Native Americans. Today, only about 100,000 survive. Many have kept their original languages, but Portuguese is spoken widely. A few tribal groups in the heart of the forest still have no contact with the modern Brazilians and are known to exist only by signs left at the edge of their territory.

Close to 40 percent of Brazilians are *mestiço,* or people of mixed racial origin. Of these, by far the largest proportion are of mixed black African and Portuguese ancestory. Others are descendants of Native Americans and Africans, and Native Americans and Europeans. All are bound together by the special national bond of beliefs, traditions, and customs that unites Brazilians.

Urban and Rural Life

More than 80 percent of Brazilians live in towns and cities. São Paulo is the largest city and home to almost 20 million people. It is second only to Mexico City as the largest metropolitan area in the world.

Brasilia, the capital of Brazil, has two million people. In contrast, much of the Amazon basin has fewer than three people per square mile (1 per sq km).

In modern Brazil, the energy of the *Paulistas*—the people of São Paulo state—is legendary. Their skill in banking and industry has created the economic powerhouse of Brazil and South America as a whole. São Paulo was founded by the Portuguese in 1554, and it was from there that organized expeditions set out into the interior. The expeditioners were known as *bandeirantes* because each group had its own *bandeira*, or flag. Some of the groups numbered up to 3,000 men. The going was tough, but they claimed vast tracts of land. The Portuguese explorers settled in small numbers to farm the interior.

Buses and cars fill the streets of the financial center in São Paulo. ▼

10

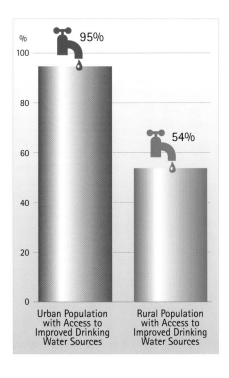

95%

54%

Urban Population with Access to Improved Drinking Water Sources

Rural Population with Access to Improved Drinking Water Sources

 A comparison of the percentage of people with access to improved drinking water sources.

Drinking Water

While most Brazilians can obtain clean drinking water, few have running water in their homes. Both urban and rural dwellers have to line up at a standpipe—a main outlet on the street—to get drinking water. In northeast Brazil in particular, some people stand in line for hours for water.

In the Amazon rain forest, many families live in houses made of timber, thatch, and palm leaves. ▼

Population movements

In the late 1500s, when natural riches were discovered in the north and along the coast, great migrations to these regions followed. In the 17th century, diamonds and gold attracted people into Minas Gerais. Wild rubber from forest trees drew thousands of migrants to the Amazon region in the late 19th century. The construction of the new capital, Brasilia, led tens of thousands more—the *candangos*—into the middle of the country in the late 1950s.

Amazonian development

A Trans-Amazon Highway project of the 1970s spurred settlement in Amazonia. A gold rush to eastern Amazonia south of Macapá occurred in the 1980s. By the end of the 20th century, the map of Brazil had changed. Fine asphalt-covered roads led to almost every corner, and modern airlines carried passengers in wide-bodied jets across the country. Today, Manaus, the Amazon regional capital, has 1.5 million inhabitants and is a thriving city.

Web Search ►►

► http://www1.ibge.gov.br/brasil_em_sintese/default.htm
A Brazilian government site showing a map of population density. Go to "Fazer download do mapa grande" to download the large map.

Farming and Fishing

Less than 50 years ago, Brazil was known for just one crop: coffee. Almost half of the world's coffee production came from there. In recent years, Brazil has developed huge agribusinesses that now account for 21 percent of its gross domestic product.

The densely populated southeast is the center for the cultivation of coffee and soy beans. Orange juice from São Paulo state is exported worldwide. Brazil has five tanker ships that are dedicated to carrying the frozen juice to the U.S. and northern Europe. Land along the coast has been cultivated for generations, and sugar cane is farmed extensively in the northeast. Fishing for local consumption is important. Large quantities of fish are caught along the coast and in the rivers.

Irrigation systems

Major irrigation systems have brought more land under cultivation. Dry land around the Rio São Francisco now produces melons, grapes, and oranges for export. The fruits are transported in specially chilled shipping containers that are taken 310 miles (500 km) by road to the coast. The huge strides in agricultural production make it appear that Brazil is simply a giant farm, but that is not the case.

Fishing

As Amazon cities and towns have grown, so has the demand for fish. Some species are becoming scarce. One of the largest freshwater fish is the pirarucu. It can weigh 308 pounds (140 kg), but most of those caught are about 66 pounds (30 kg), and even that size is declining around markets such as Manaus and Belém. Along the coast, fishermen work with many types of small boats. The catches include shrimp, crabs, lobsters, corvina, swordfish, and shark. Most shellfish are sold in local markets, but some are exported.

Mechanized farming in São Paulo state. Here, corn is being cut to make silage, a food for farm animals. ▼

Cattle ranching is a major industry in the central and southern plateau regions. Cowboys in southern Brazil are known as *gauchos*.

Local production

Small-scale farmers still work for the local markets. Some have two acres (1 ha) or less of land and barely make a living from growing fruit or root crops.

In the rural areas, most homes have space for growing only their own root crops. The majority of Native Americans have gardens for growing age-old natural crops such as mandioca (manioc or cassava). Native Americans also catch fish in the rivers. Baited hooks and nylon lines are replacing the old methods of bows and arrows and fish traps.

Farming

The south and coastal region are the main agricultural areas.

Brasilia

Cattle
Pigs
Sheep
Citrus Fruit
Coffee
Cotton
Soy Beans
Sugar Cane
Timber

Pasture
Cropland
Forest

Web Search ►►

► http://www.ibge.
gov.br

The Brazilian Statistics Institute site has farming and fishing statistics that are updated every three months. There is also news about the problems faced by Brazilian farmers and fishermen.

Resources and Industry

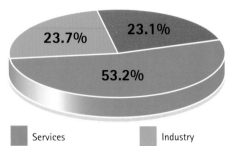

23.1%

23.7%

53.2%

■ Services ■ Industry

■ Agriculture

▲ Proportion of the workforce in the three main areas of employment in Brazil.

At the Carajás open-cast mine, huge mechanical shovels are used to gather iron ore for export or for processing in foundries within Brazil. ▼

During the 20th century, Brazil changed from a purely agricultural producer to an industrialized nation in a series of leaps. One of the greatest leaps was during the 1970s when, by using loans from abroad, industry took off dramatically.

Much of the development has brought changes to the environment. In 1986, production at the enormous Carajás iron deposits in eastern Amazonia began, and a railway 550 miles (890 km) long was built to carry the ore to the coast. Large areas of rain forest were destroyed to make way for the railroad, and increased mining polluted many rivers.

São Paulo expanded to become an industrial heartland. In its factories today, vehicles are produced for domestic use and export. The country has its own aircraft industry and exports small passenger planes. The supermarkets are filled with goods "Made in Brazil."

The Environment

Brazil holds the key to the greatest rain forest preserves in the world.

Environmentalists believe that expansion into the Amazon basin will destroy the forest, so protective measures have been taken. Large national parks and forest preserves have been established, and elsewhere there are some controls on the way the forest is used. Programs to replant trees cut down for timber are actively promoted.

Energy

Brazil has its own oil reserves that are mainly offshore to the southeast of Rio de Janeiro. Energy also comes from coal, gas, and hydropower. One of the world's largest hydroelectric plants, Itaipú, was completed on the Paraná River in 1985. Gas for the energy-hungry São Paulo region is imported from neighboring Bolivia along a 1,960-mile (3,150 km) long pipeline opened in 2001.

Encouraging industry

One of the most enterprising of all the economic ideas of the 1950s was the creation of a free trade zone around Manaus in Amazonia. Special tax laws apply there, and many companies, especially in electronics, have set up factories. Goods made in Manaus are then exported to the rest of Brazil, South America, and places worldwide. Many of the workers are women, and each day chartered buses take them from their homes to the factories.

A car factory assembly line. Many of the cars built in Brazil are exported around the world. ▼

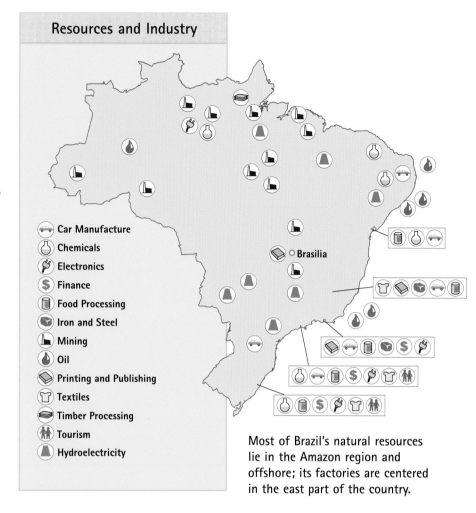

Resources and Industry

- 🚗 Car Manufacture
- 🧪 Chemicals
- ⚡ Electronics
- $ Finance
- 🥫 Food Processing
- ⚙ Iron and Steel
- ⛏ Mining
- 🛢 Oil
- 📘 Printing and Publishing
- 👕 Textiles
- 📚 Timber Processing
- 👥 Tourism
- 🔺 Hydroelectricity

Most of Brazil's natural resources lie in the Amazon region and offshore; its factories are centered in the east part of the country.

Web Search ►►

► http://www.suframa.gov.br
To learn more about the extraordinary "Zona Franca" in the middle of the Amazon rain forest , try the official site.

► http://www.embratur.gov.br
This site set up by the Brazilian Tourist Office has a good "Children's Corner."

Transportation

For a country the size of Brazil, a good transportation system is essential. For the first European settlers, the interior was almost inaccessible. They used the rivers, particularly in Amazonia, until trails were cut through the forests.

The first railway line was built in 1852 and was soon followed by lines reaching inland from the coast. Then proper roads were built, and these were improved during the 1970s and '80s with super-highways, some of them thousands of miles long.

Bus travel

Long-distance travel is mostly on buses. At the top end of the market is the *Expresso luxo,* or luxury express. These buses have air-conditioning, sleeper seats, and television. At the cheaper end, most services are comfortable and reliable. Virtually every town has an *estação rodoviária,* or bus station. The best have monitor screens with schedules, ticket offices, showers, restaurants, and shops. A journey from Brasilia to Belém at the mouth of the Amazon may take two days. Tickets—with assigned seating—are bought in advance, luggage is checked, and the bus stops at most towns along the way.

Cars and underground railways

Cars—even old ones—are a luxury and are owned only by well-paid office, factory, or professional workers. Everyone else uses the local buses or taxis. Rio de Janeiro and São Paulo have modern, efficient subway systems. Curitiba—a city in the south—prides itself on its environmentally sound transportation. Buses use special routes, and there are small, covered passenger stations on the sidewalk where tickets are bought before boarding.

Air transportation

Wealthy Brazilians, or those who have borrowed from friends and family, usually choose to fly the long distances within the country. Brazilian airlines have modern jets, and major airports are of a high standard. Hundreds of minor towns and settlements have smaller airports that are often no more than a hut beside a dirt runway. They are used by regional airlines using propeller aircraft carrying a dozen passengers or fewer.

Ways to Travel

Some curiosities of early transportation have survived. Part of the Rio de Janeiro tramway system runs between the old city center and the hillside suburb of Santa Teresa. In Salvador, which is built on a hill, the upper and lower parts of the town are connected by a funicular railway—two steeply inclined tracks carrying cabins which are hauled up or down by cables.

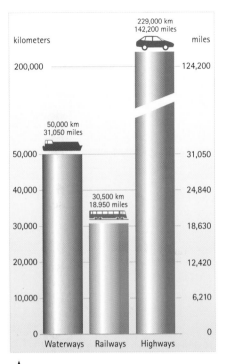

kilometers

229,000 km
142,200 miles

miles

200,000 — 124,200

50,000 km
31,050 miles

50,000 — 31,050

40,000 — 24,840

30,500 km
18.950 miles

30,000 — 18,630

20,000 — 12,420

10,000 — 6,210

0 — 0

Waterways   Railways   Highways

A comparison of the lengths of the main transportation systems.

Many cars run on alcohol that is derived from sugar cane.

Transportation

Amapá
Manaus ✈   Santarém   Belém ✈
Fortaleza ✈
Marabá   Teresina
Rio Branco   Porto Velho   Recife
Juazeiro   Maceió
Salvador
Cuiabá   Brasília
Montes Claros
Campo   São José do   Belo Horizonte ✈
Grande   Rio Preto
Marília
Rio de Janeiro ✈
São Paulo ✈
Curitiba
Porto Alegre ✈

✈ Major Airport
〜 Highways
〜 Main Roads
〜 Railways

Major road and rail routes are concentrated in the east.

Web Search ►►

► http://www.varig.com. br/english/index.htm
The site of Varig, the Brazilian national airline.

► http://www.mp.usp. br.mamore.htm
From the Museum of São Paulo, this shows the "Devil's Railway" of the 1800s that survives in parts of the Amazon forest.

Education

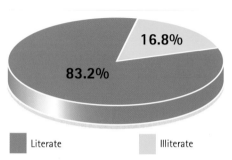

■ Literate ■ Illiterate

▲ The percentages of people in Brazil who are able or unable to read and write.

A village school built on the banks of a river in Amazonia. The building is raised off the ground to avoid flood damage. ▼

Approximately one in five Brazilians are school age. Most children attend school from age 7 to age 14. Some continue in secondary (high) school until they are 18. A few do not attend school at all, and about 20 percent of the population cannot read or write.

The state provides many schools, and others are run by churches. Many schools, especially in the cities, may be private, with families paying tuition. At the secondary level, classroom space is often limited, and students attend in shifts. This system helps the school and also gives the students time to work to earn money.

At the age of 18, pupils take an exam to qualify for college. There are many universities. University graduates may go directly to work in Brazil. A lucky few will find scholarships for graduate school or to do research in other countries. Brazil produces fine surgeons, scientists, and other professionals.

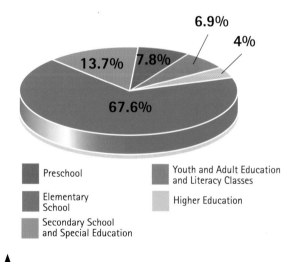

■ Preschool
■ Elementary School
■ Secondary School and Special Education
■ Youth and Adult Education and Literacy Classes
■ Higher Education

▲ Proportions of students in the various educational establishments in Brazil.

Universities

Many students have to leave home to study at distant universities. Some live with local families. Many parents work extra hours to ensure that their children get a better education than was possible when they were young.

At every level of education, the environment is a national issue. Non-government organizations raise money from businesses or by selling T-shirts and books to fund their educational programs.

▲ Pupils in a classroom in a state-run primary school in Caerá, northeast Brazil.

Providing for an education

In rural communities, classes begin early in the day and finish at midday. This gives children time to help their parents work on the land or at their crafts. Even small villages have two or sometimes three schools to which the children walk or travel by public bus.

Cities have state-run schools in each area, and most pupils walk to school. Schools in towns and cities have the advantage that Brazil is well-equipped with museums and places that hold exhibitions. Some pupils have the chance to visit these educational centers as part of their studies.

Radio, television, and the Internet now carry education to many more people. The Brazilian government, institutions, and many companies have children's or teen pages on their Internet sites. Some newspapers and magazines are extremely aware of their responsibilities and have well-illustrated educational sections.

  Web Search ►►

► http://www.inep.gov. br/idiomas/ingles.htm
This site includes downloadable files of the National Education Plan and exam samples.

► http://www.stpauls.br/
A long-established private school in São Paulo—the site is in English and has pictures of the school.

► http://www.unb.br/
The showcase university of the capital city, opened in the 1960s.

► http://www.inpa.gov.br
The National Amazon Research Institute site is in Portuguese but has an English version under construction.

Sports and Leisure

Soccer

Brazil has 35 major soccer teams. Rio de Janeiro has the famous Maracana Stadium, with seating for 125,000 and standing room for 30,000. It has slipped in world size ranking to third, but it still holds the record for the 199,854 spectators who watched the World Cup final in 1950. Brazil has won the World Cup five times. Edson Arantes do Nascimento, or Pele, is Brazil's most famous soccer star. In his career, he played 1,362 games, scoring an incredible 1,280 goals.

Above all other sports, Brazilians are dedicated to soccer. Go out on a Brazilian street on the day of a big soccer match and it will be empty while everyone is glued to the television. Go out on the same street if the home team loses and it will be filled with gloom.

Car racing is a close second in popularity, followed by volleyball, tennis, basketball, swimming, and bicycling. Many younger Brazilians with some money to spend are involved in outdoor activities such as hiking, climbing, and sailing.

The Brazilian Olympic team won 12 medals in the 2000 games in Sydney, Australia. Brazilian athletes also compete in the PanAmerican games held every four years. Most large towns have special facilities for disabled athletes, and the country sends teams to compete in world paraplegic events. Sixty-four wheelchair athletes went to the Sydney Paralympic Games in 2000 and won 22 medals.

Playing volleyball on the beach at Rio de Janeiro. In the background is Sugar Loaf Mountain (shown on the cover of this book). ▼▼

Leisure time

Chess is played in homes, community halls, parks, and by the beach. Brazil has an annual chess championship and competes internationally. For the more active, there are hiking groups and groups for kayaking, paragliding, and ultralight flying. Climbing is restricted to places with cliffs or big rocks such as those around Rio de Janeiro. Horseback riding is popular in both urban and rural areas.

The Maracana soccer stadium in Rio de Janeiro, the third-largest in the world.

Car racing

Rio de Janeiro and São Paulo have internationally famous car racing tracks—the Jacarepaguá and Interlagos, respectively. They take turns holding the Formula One Brazilian Grand Prix.

Three Brazilian drivers—Emerson Fittipaldi, Nelson Piquet, and Ayrton Senna—dominated the Formula One events for 30 years. Fittipaldi was the winner of the Driver's Championship twice in the 1970s, Piquet won it three times in the '80s, and Senna was the star of the 1990s. He won the Driver's Championship three times. When Senna died in a car racing accident in Italy in 1994, the entire country was in mourning for days.

Web Search ▶▶

▶ http://www.futbrasil. com/arquivo/rankings/ placar.html
A list of the Brazilian soccer teams and their rankings.

▶ http://www.360soccer. com/pele
Read about the career of Pele— Edson Arantes do Nascimento —the world's greatest soccer player.

▶ http://www.senna. globo.com/instituto ayrtonsenna
This organization, set up by Ayrton Senna, helps young people across Brazil; the site is only in Portuguese.

Daily Life and Religion

On Easter Day 1500, Portuguese explorers landed on the Atlantic coast of South America near a hill they named *Monte Pascoal,* or Easter Hill. The country they named *Santa Cruz,* or Good Cross, but that was soon changed to Brazil.

The explorers brought with them the Catholic religion, and today small wayside chapels are still known by the old name of *Santa-Cruz.* The Native Americans whom the explorers encountered had their own simple religion based on forest spirits, the earth, and the sky. The Europeans soon converted them to Catholicism. Then came the black African slaves with their own religion, some of which has survived. Immigrants brought other faiths to the country.

Today in Brazil, evangelical churches—especially from North America—are having a profound effect in some cities. In São Paulo, where life is stressful for many and without hope for many more, the evangelical churches have converted millions of people. Radio is important for spreading the teachings of these churches.

DATABASE

Armed forces

Brazil has a navy, air force, and army. They have separate command centers in each major region run by career officers. All Brazilian men must complete 12 months' military training beginning at age 19. Some people are exempted because of their religious beliefs, studies, or careers. Brazilian women do not have to do military training.

A papier mâché figure of Judas Iscariot is carried through the streets during a Holy Week parade. ▼

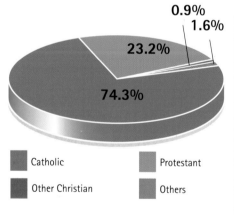

0.9%
1.6%
23.2%
74.3%

- Catholic
- Other Christian
- Protestant
- Others

▲ Members of the major faiths in Brazil. Most Brazilians are Catholic, as are the majority of South Americans.

For the Carnival in Rio de Janeiro, performers appear in stunning costumes.

The work week

Brazilians do not all work the same hours. Many stores in the southeast may not open until 9:00 or even 10:00 A.M., but they close late in the day. In the heat of Amazonia, some stores close at midday and then stay open until 10:00 P.M. Local markets open soon after dawn. Offices often open early and close when the work is finished. Traffic in São Paulo is heavy all night, and the first commuter flight for Rio de Janeiro leaves before 7:00 A.M. Sundays are for leisure.

Healthcare

Free healthcare is available to every Brazilian, funded by the tax system. Towns and cities have hospitals, and in rural areas there is usually a medical clinic. A national vaccination program exists for young children. Brazil produces large quantities of pharmaceuticals for domestic and export markets. Many wealthy Brazilians pay for private healthcare treatment.

Carnival

Carnival (*Carnaval* in Portuguese) is a time of great happiness and enjoyment for Brazilians. It is held on the weekend before Ash Wednesday, the beginning of the Christian period of Lent, but the modern festival seems to have little connection with religion.

Web Search ►►

► http://www.nova jerusalem.com.br
Looks at the Easter passion play, The Suffering of Christ, at Nova Jerusalem in northeast Brazil.

► http://www.brasilia convention.com.br/ english/default.asp
Site of the Brasilia Convention Center, which has stores, theaters, and exhibitions.

Arts and Media

Brazil is a media country where television draws massive audiences. Satellites beam channels to every region. Music is full of rhythm and very "Brazilian"—noisy, lively, and melodic. It is followed by a wide audience outside the country. Live concerts fill arenas, beaches, and theaters.

Away from the intensely youthful modern Brazil, there is a strong cultural tradition supported by world famous writers, composers, musicians, and filmmakers.

The Brazilian media giant *Globo* runs a leading newspaper and the country's most successful television channel, *Rede Globo,* or Globo Network. The channel owns 113 transmitters covering 99.85 percent of the 5,443 municipalities, or local areas, in Brazil. Some television programs have audiences of over 120 million.

Editora Abril in São Paulo is a huge publishing house of books and magazines. One of its best-known magazines, *Veja,* has a circulation of 1.2 million, and delivery trucks drive 93,225 miles (150,000 km) a week to distribute it.

Writers

Some Brazilian writers are international names. Jorge Amado from Salvador wrote 30 novels, many using themes from the deep-rooted Afro-Brazilian culture of the northeast. Gilberto Freyre wrote classics about Brazilian social history, especially the sugar plantation era in the 18th and 19th centuries.

Music

Brazilian dance music is known around the world, and the beat of the *samba* is the sound of carnival. It has its roots in African culture. Northeastern Brazil produces many of the country's best singers. Perhaps the best-known piece of Brazilian classical music is *Bachianas Brasileiras* by renowned composer Heitor Villa Lobos.

◄◄ The Opera House in Manaus.

24

Newspapers and magazines

The media cover the country. For example, Rio Branco, on an Amazon tributary, is 1,680 miles (2,700 km) from São Paulo and has a population of 253,000. Today it is best-known for the time in 1988 when Chico Mendes, a forest rubber tapper trying to save the environment, was assassinated by land developers in a nearby town. Rio Branco has its own paper, *O Rio Branco*, and a local TV station. The newspaper and the TV schedules can be found on-line. Air services deliver other newspapers and magazines from the southeast.

Famous films

The list of Brazilian film names begins with the vivacious Carmen Miranda, who rose to fame in the 1930s and '40s with 19 films. More recently, a young director from Rio de Janeiro, Walter Salles, has won international acclaim for his work, which includes *Central Station* and *Behind the Sun*, both set in northeastern Brazil.

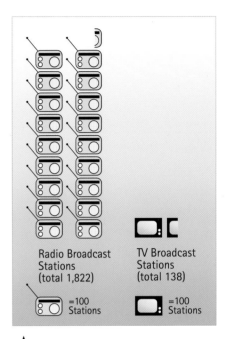

Radio Broadcast Stations (total 1,822)

TV Broadcast Stations (total 138)

= 100 Stations

= 100 Stations

▲ Brazil has a vast number of local radio and TV stations.

Growth in number of foreign tourists visiting Brazil. ▼

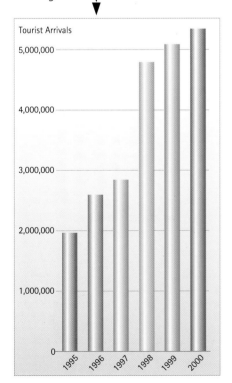

Tourist Arrivals

5,000,000

4,000,000

3,000,000

2,000,000

1,000,000

0

1995 1996 1997 1998 1999 2000

DATABASE

Tourism

Embratur, the official Brazilian tourism organization, has for many years promoted the country as a tourist paradise, and world interest is growing, especially for wilderness trips. In the far west part of the country, the Pantanal—a huge swamp rich with wildlife—is a popular destination. Brazilian beaches are another magnet, and particularly in the south there are resort developments attracting visitors from Argentina and Uruguay.

Web Search ▶▶

▶ http://www.lyngsat.com/brasilb1.shtml
See the channels and areas covered by a satellite parked in orbit above Brazil.

▶ http://www.uol.com.br/criancas/vejakid.htm
Site of the children's version of the magazine Veja *in Portuguese.*

▶ http://www.uol.com.br/allbrazilianmusic
All Brazilian Music, *the music from Brazil (in English).*

Government

Brazil is a democratic republic—its full name is the Federative Republic of Brazil. There are 26 states and one federal district which surrounds Brasilia, the capital. Each state has a governor and its own administration for local affairs.

Each state sends elected representatives to the National Congress in Brasilia. The president is the head of state and leads the country from the capital. The presidential palace is the *Planalto Palace*, but the president's house is separate from this.

Brazil declared independence from Portugal on September 7, 1822, and has gone through some difficult times to reach its present constitution with an elected government. Most recently, Brazil was ruled by the military from 1964 to 1985, when elections were resumed. All Brazilians between the ages of 18 and 70 must vote. Presidential elections are held every four years, and the president may run for a second term.

The Palace of Congress in Brasilia. ▼

Congress

The National Congress consists of two chambers. A senate of 81 seats is made up of elected members from each state and the federal district. The Chamber of Deputies, also elected from the individual states, has 513 members. The president appoints the cabinet that controls the nation's affairs, including economic, foreign, health, and educational policies. Government departments and institutions implement the policies and make suggestions for changes.

Justice

The highest court in Brazil is the Supreme Federal Tribunal of 11 ministers appointed by the president and confirmed by the senate. Below this there is a Supreme Tribunal of Justice responsible for the ordinary laws. Regional federal tribunals are composed of at least seven judges, usually from the local area. There are special military tribunals for cases of crime in the armed forces.

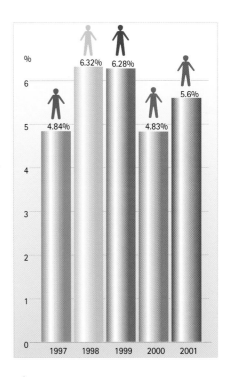

▲ In recent years, about 1 in 20 workers are unemployed.

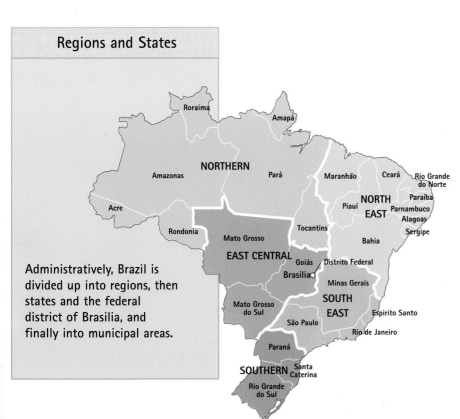

Regions and States

Administratively, Brazil is divided up into regions, then states and the federal district of Brasilia, and finally into municipal areas.

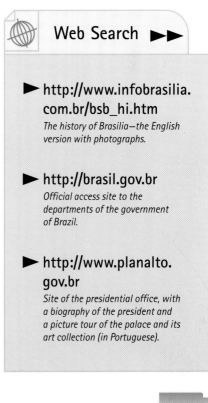

Web Search ▶▶

▶ http://www.infobrasilia.com.br/bsb_hi.htm
The history of Brasilia—the English version with photographs.

▶ http://brasil.gov.br
Official access site to the departments of the government of Brazil.

▶ http://www.planalto.gov.br
Site of the presidential office, with a biography of the president and a picture tour of the palace and its art collection (in Portuguese).

Place in the World

Brazil is known for its music, soccer, and carnivals. Beyond that popular image, it has an even stronger place in the world as the largest South American nation, the world's eighth-largest economy, and a partner in *Mercosur*—a regional trading organization that is the world's fourth-largest economic market.

Brazil hosted the great world environmental conference in 1992—the Earth Summit—and has signed all the major environmental agreements.

Economic giant

Brazil is a giant among Latin American countries. The value of its exports and imports virtually balance. Progress is slowed only by the way the income is shared within the country and the debt owed to foreign banks.

In 2002, almost 20 percent of the population were living below the poverty line. At times in the recent past, the economy has been affected by severe inflation, and in 1992 the currency was changed from the *cruzado* to the *real* in a meticulously planned operation that brought stability and helped the Brazilian image overseas. Trade grew, and more and more people around the world have found Brazilian goods in their stores.

$58.9 billion
(Transport equipment, metallurgical products, soy beans, bran, oils, chemicals, iron ore, coffee)

EXPORTS

IMPORTS

$61.4 billion
(Machinery and equipment, electrical equipment, chemicals, oil, electricity)

◄◄ A comparison of the value and content of Brazil's imports and exports.

Position in South America

Brazil's independence from Portugal in September 1822 came at a time when many of the neighboring countries were winning independence from Spain by war. Brazil declared independence and moved forward with Prince Pedro, the heir to the Portuguese throne, as the head of state. This smooth transition helped Brazil to prosper while other South American countries struggled.

Modern Brazil, with strongly nationalistic and tolerant citizens, soon came to be seen as the land of the future. The people have not changed, but regional circumstances have, and Brazil now faces two challenges—rising domestic poverty and finding new markets for trade.

Images of Native Americans in Brazil, such as this Yanomami Indian, have created global awareness of the destruction of the rain forests. ▼

DATABASE

Chronology of Historical Events from 1962

1964–84
Military rule

1984
After the sudden death of Tancredo Neves, the president-elect, Vice President José Sarney takes office

1994
The "Plan Real" of Finance Minister Fernando Henrique Cardoso successfully controls severe inflation

1995
Cardoso becomes president; during the 1990s, worldwide economic chaos affected the stability of the real

 Web Search ▶▶

▶ http://www.lanic.utexas.edu/la.brazil/economy/
The University of Texas has a service in English known as LANIC that offers coverage of the Brazilian economy and development.

▶ http://www.guia-mercosur.com/
Tables and charts about the trading organization Mercosur—the member countries and its future plans.

▶ http://www.europa.eu.int/comm/external_relations/mercosur/intro/index.htm
Site highlighting the European Union's links with Mercosur.

Area:
3,286,473 square miles
(8,511,965 sq km)

Population size:
175,572,000

Capital city:
Brasilia (population 2.1 million
including the federal district)

Other major cities:
São Paulo (metropolitan area
18.3 million), Rio de Janeiro
(6 million), Belo Horizonte
(2.2 million), Manaus (1.4 million)

Longest national river:
Rio São Francisco (1,965 miles
(3,161 km)). The Amazon River
(1,963 miles (3,158 km) in Brazil),
is not totally Brazilian.

Highest mountain:
Pico da Neblina (9,888 feet
(3,014 m))

Currency:
Real (plural Reis)

Flag:
The flag is green with a large
yellow diamond in the center
bearing a blue celestial globe with

27 white, five-pointed stars. The
stars represent the states of Brazil
and the federal district. The globe
has a white, equator-like band with
the motto *Ordem e Progresso*—Order
and Progess. November 19 is the Day
of the Flag and is marked with a
moment of silence at noon.

Language:
Official: Portuguese
Others include Native American
languages

Natural resources:
Bauxite, iron ore, manganese, nickel,
phosphates, platinum, tin, uranium,
petroleum, hydropower, timber

Major exports:
Agricultural products, food products,
steel, motor vehicles, aircraft,
machinery, timber, tin and aluminum
ore, textiles, shoes, pharmaceuticals.

**Some national holidays and
festivals:**
New Year's Day (January 1)
Carnaval (February or March,
   four days before Ash
   Wednesday)
Tiradentes Day (April 21)
Labor Day (May 1)
Independence Day (September 7)
Our Lady of the Aparecida
   (October 12)
Proclamation of the Republic
   (November 15)
Immaculate Conception
   (December 8)
Christmas Day (December 25)
Individual states may have their
own additional holidays.

Official religion:
80 percent nominally Roman
Catholic. Other religions include
Protestant, Buddhist, Afro-
Brazilian, and Native American.

Glossary

AMAZONIA
That part of Brazil drained by the Amazon River.

CARNAVAL
Portuguese for "carnival"—a pre-Lent festival celebration, like Mardi Gras.

COLONIES
Countries or territories taken over or ruled by other countries.

DEMOCRATIC
Based on democracy—a form of government in which the power rests with the will of the people.

DEPUTIES (CHAMBER OF)
People appointed to act on behalf of the individual states.

ECONOMY
The basis on which a country's wealth is organized.

ENVIRONMENT
The natural world including wildlife, oceans, landscape, and the atmosphere.

EXPORTS
Goods and services sold by a country to other countries.

FEDERAL GOVERNMENT
A form of government in which two or more states work together while maintaining some independence.

GROSS DOMESTIC PRODUCT (GDP)
The value of all the goods and services produced by a country over a year or other period.

HYDROELECTRIC POWER
Electricity generated from the energy of water movement.

IMMIGRANT
A person from one country who enters another country to live there.

IMPORTS
Goods and services bought by a country from other countries.

INDEPENDENCE
Governing of a country by its own people.

LIFE EXPECTANCY
The age to which someone may be expected to live.

MERCOSUR/MERCOSUL
A South American trading organization. The name is shortened from Spanish/Portuguese for Southern Market. Current members are Argentina, Uruguay, Brazil, and Paraguay.

NATIVE AMERICANS
The original inhabitants of the American continents. Brazilians say *povos indigenas*—indigenous peoples.

PAULISTA/PAULISTANO
A person from the state or city of São Paulo.

REPUBLIC
An independent country whose head of state is an elected president.

SATELLITE
An object in orbit around a planet.

STATE
A body or unit that is responsible for its affairs. Individual states in Brazil have independent powers within the framework of the federal government.

Index